Hey, Pearl?
What, Wagner?
Knock Knock!
Who's there?
Ice Cream!
Ice Cream, who?

Ice Cream
when I ride a
roller coaster!

Pearl and Wagner
Three Secrets

by Kate McMullan
pictures by R. W. Alley

Dial Books for Young Readers • New York

Published by Dial Books for Young Readers ★ A division of Penguin Young Readers Group ★ 345 Hudson Street ★ New York, New York 10014 ★ Manufactured in China on acid-free paper ★ The Dial Easy-to-Read logo is a registered trademark of Dial Books for Young Readers, a division of Penguin Young Readers Group ★ ® TM 1,162,718. ★ Library of Congress Cataloging-in-Publication Data ★ McMullan, Kate. ★ Pearl and Wagner : three secrets / by Kate McMullan ; pictures by R. W. Alley. ★ p. cm. ★ "Dial Easy-to-Read." ★ Summary: Pearl and Wagner, a rabbit and a mouse who are best friends, learn about secrets during a trip to an ice cream factory and an amusement park birthday party. ★ ISBN 0-8037-2574-4 ★ [1. Ice cream—Fiction. 2. Amusement parks—Fiction. 3. Roller coasters—Fiction. 4. Secrets—Fiction. 5. Birthdays—Fiction. 6. Rabbits—Fiction. 7. Mice—Fiction.] I. Alley, R. W. (Robert W.), ill. II. Title. ★ PZ7.M2295 Pdt 2004 ★ [E]—dc21 ★ 2002153680 ★ Reading Level 2.0 ★ 10 9 8 7 6 5 4 3 2 1

The art was created using pen and ink, watercolor,
and a few colored pencils on Strathmore Bristol.

For Bob, who created
the world's greatest Zoomer

—K.M.

For Chuck and Jeffrey,
my third-grade pals

—R.W.A.

CONTENTS

Oo Pp Qq Rr Ss Tt Uu
TODAY: FIELD TRIP
MILK
CREAM
SUGAR
FLAVOR
FACTORY
ICE CREAM
Ice Cream World!
WATCH IT BEING MADE!
Free Samples!
over 200 flavors
digital cones

Ms. Star's class was going to visit an ice cream factory.

"I love ice cream," said Pearl.

"I dream about it," said Wagner.

Everyone lined up for the bus.

"Save me a place, Wag," said Pearl.

She ran to get her jacket.

Lulu got in line behind Wagner.

"Want to know a secret?" she said.

"No," said Wagner.

"Secrets are too hard to keep."

But Lulu told him the secret anyway.

Pearl came back.

She saw Lulu whispering to Wagner.

Pearl and Wagner sat down in the bus.

"What did Lulu say?" Pearl asked.

"I can't tell you," said Wagner.

"It's a secret."

"Oh," said Pearl.

Wagner felt awful.

The bus pulled up

to the ice cream factory.

"Wow!" said Henry.

"This place looks like

a giant ice cream cone!"

"Lulu won't mind if you tell me,"

said Pearl.

"I can't," said Wagner.

He felt even worse.

The class went inside.

They saw a large vat of cream.

Big paddles were stirring it.

"Oh, boy!" said Bud.

"Did you promise not to tell?"

said Pearl.

"Not exactly," said Wagner.

A machine poured mint into the cream.

Another machine added

chocolate chips.

"Yum!" said Henry.

"Then tell me," said Pearl.

"I shouldn't," said Wagner.

A machine poured the ice cream

into boxes.

The boxes went into a big freezer.

“Brrrr!” said Bud.

“Give me a hint,” said Pearl.

“It wouldn’t be right,” said Wagner.

The last stop was the Tasting Room.

Everyone got a double-dip cone.

"Tell me the first word," said Pearl.

Wagner put his hands over his mouth.

He shook his head.

Lulu came by, licking her cone.

"Aren't you having any?" she asked.

"Wagner won't tell me your secret,"

said Pearl.

"I'm having a birthday party," said Lulu.

"That's not a secret!" said Pearl.

"I know about your party."

"Wagner didn't," said Lulu.

"It was a secret to him."

"Secrets," said Wagner.

"Phooey!"

“Time to go, class!” said Ms. Star.

“Wait!” said Wagner.

“I didn’t look around.”

“I didn’t get any ice cream!” said Pearl.

“Next time,” said Ms. Star.

Everyone got back on the bus.

Pearl and Wagner could not believe

they had missed the ice cream.

“Don’t worry,” said Ms. Star.

“We have another class trip next week.”

“Where?” said Wagner.

“I’ll keep that a secret,” said Ms. Star.

Lulu sent everyone in the class an invitation.

“We will all ride the bumper cars,”

Lulu told everyone.

“We will all ride the tea cups.

We will all ride the Zoomer.”

“What is the Zoomer?” asked Wagner.

“The Zoomer is a roller coaster,”

said Lulu.

“It is the biggest, fastest,

scariest roller coaster ever.”

“Oh,” said Wagner.

"I am wearing my new red hat
to Lulu's party,"
Pearl told Wagner at recess.
"What are you wearing?"

"I'm not going," said Wagner.

"WHAT?" said Pearl. "Why not?"

"I have to get my teeth cleaned,"

said Wagner.

"You did that last week," said Pearl.

"I have to buy new socks," said Wagner.

"Tell me the real reason," said Pearl.

"It's a secret," said Wagner.

"I won't tell," said Pearl.

"I hate roller coasters," said Wagner.

"Have you ever been
on a roller coaster?" said Pearl.

Wagner shook his head.

"The cars go too high," he said.

"They come down too fast.
And they are way too loud."

"Lulu's party won't be any fun
without you, Wagner," said Pearl.
"I am going to help you.
When I am done,
you will love roller coasters."

"Don't count on it," said Wagner.

Pearl and Wagner climbed to the top of the jungle gym.

"You are up high now," said Pearl.

"How do you feel?"

"Not bad," said Wagner.

Pearl took Wagner over to the slide.

"Slide down as fast as you can,"

she told him.

Wagner zoomed down the slide.

"How do you feel?" said Pearl.

"Fine," said Wagner.

Pearl took Wagner over to the fence.

Workers on the other side of it

were using a jack hammer.

RAT-A-TAT! RAT-A-TAT!

"THIS IS LOUD,"

Pearl yelled over the noise.

"HOW DO YOU FEEL?"

"DANDY!" yelled Wagner.

"One more thing," said Pearl.

"Say this to yourself over and over.

'I rule the roller coaster!'"

"I rule the roller coaster!" said Wagner.

"Say it like you mean it," said Pearl.

Wagner said,

"I RULE THE

ROLLER COASTER!"

"Who rules?" said Pearl.

"ME!" said Wagner. "I DO!"

"You're ready," said Pearl.

"Bring on the Zoomer!" said Wagner.

On Saturday, Pearl and Wagner
went to Ride-o-Rama.
They gave their presents for Lulu
to Lulu's mom.
Then they ran to the bumper cars.

"Let's drive!" said Lulu.

Bam! Wagner bumped Bud.

Bam! Bud bumped Pearl.

Bam! Pearl bumped Lulu.

BAM! Lulu bumped Henry.

"Yikes!" said Henry.

"What fun!" yelled Lulu.

Everyone raced for the tea cups.

They got in and sat down.

The tea cups started spinning.

They spun faster and faster.

When the ride was over,

everyone was good and dizzy.

“To the Zoomer!” yelled Lulu.

Pearl and Wagner ran over
to the roller coaster.

"Who rules?" said Pearl.
"I do!" said Wagner.
"Pearl! Wagner!" called Lulu.
"That is the Little Duck
roller coaster.
The Zoomer is over here!"

Pearl and Wagner looked up
at the Zoomer.
It was as tall as a skyscraper.
It had lots of really big hills.
"I rule the roller coaster!"
said Wagner.
Pearl swallowed.

Henry and Lulu got into a car.
A man pulled a bar down
in front of them.

Pearl and Wagner were next.
"I'm ready!" said Wagner.
"I'm not going," said Pearl.

"WHAT?" said Wagner. "Why not?"

"I have to get a drink of water," said Pearl.

"You can do that later," said Wagner.

"My hat might fly off," said Pearl.

"Tell me the real reason," said Wagner.

"It's a secret," said Pearl.

"I won't tell," said Wagner.

"I'm scared!" said Pearl.

“Next!” called the man.

Wagner sat down in the car.

“Come on, Pearl,” he said.

“I will help you.”

Pearl sat down next to Wagner.

The man pulled the bar down

in front of them.

"Good-bye, Wagner," said Pearl.

"It's been nice knowing you."

"Let's zoom!" yelled Lulu.

The roller coaster

rolled up the first hill.

"I am going to be sick," said Pearl.

"I have a better idea," said Wagner.

"What?" said Pearl.

"Scream!" said Wagner.

The roller coaster raced down the hill.

Pearl screamed.

Wagner screamed.

Everyone on the roller coaster

screamed like crazy.

Z

They flew up the hills.

They shot down the hills.

They zoomed around the curves.

They raced down the track

and stopped.

The man lifted the bar.

"Over so soon?" said Wagner.

Pearl and Wagner got out of the car.

"Let's go again!" said Pearl.

Lulu looked a little green.

"Let's have presents first," she said.

Lulu opened her presents.

Then everyone sang "Happy Birthday."

Lulu blew out seven candles.

Pearl asked for three scoops
of ice cream on her cake.
“I love ice cream!” said Pearl.

“That’s no secret,” said Wagner.
He sang, “You scream, I scream,
we all scream for ice cream!”

After their cake,
the two friends rode the Zoomer
until it was time to go home.